OUTSIDE,

INSIDE

BY Carolyn Crimi

ILLUSTRATED BY

Linnea Asplind Riley

SCHOLASTIC INC.
New York Toronto London Auckland Sydney

ISBN 0-590-86881-0

Text copyright © 1995 by Carolyn Crimi.
Illustrations copyright © 1995 by Linnea Asplind Riley.
All rights reserved. Published by Scholastic Inc., 555 Broadway, New York, NY 10012,
by arrangement with Simon & Schuster Children's Publishing Division.

12 11 10 9 8 7 6 5 4 3 2   6 7 8 9/9 0 1/0

Printed in the U.S.A.   08

First Scholastic printing, September 1996

To my parents, for all their love and encouragement

—CC

Outside, black clouds
sink down to the bottom
of the sky.

Inside, Molly stretches
and yawns in her
red flannel robe.

Outside, tree leaves flap in the crying wind.

Inside, Molly's slippers whisper down the hall.

Outside, a worried rabbit darts across the lawn.

Inside, Molly's cat sleeps beneath the needlepoint footstool.

Outside, the rain spills
from the clouds,
shussh-wissh,
shussh-wissh,
shussh-wissh.

Inside, the clock ticks

in the hall,

tink-tunk,

tink-tunk,

tink-tunk.

Outside, puddles bubble and churn with the falling rain.

Inside, maple syrup slips down a pancake mountain.

Outside, a slash of lightning
scratches the sky.

Inside, a spark streaks
out of the fireplace.

Outside, rain rushes over shiny, wet rocks.

Inside, Molly's cat's-eye marbles skim across the hardwood floor.

Outside, thunder stomps over the hills and meadows.

Inside, Molly twirls

on her tiptoes.

Outside, the rain slows down, plop...plop...plop.

Inside, Molly counts the raindrops rolling down the windowpane.

Outside, the garden oozes

with gloppy, sloshy mud.

Inside, Molly squishes fresh cookie dough between her fingers.

Outside, a sparrow shakes the rain from his feathers.

Inside, Molly's cat arches his back after his morning nap.

Outside, the sun pushes through a crack in the clouds.

Inside, Molly swings the door open . . .

and lets the outside in!